I DON'T LIKE TO READ!

NANCY CARLSON

PUFFIN BOOKS

Dedicated to the libraries of Edina, Minnesota,
where I got my start as a lifelong reader.

PUFFIN BOOKS
Published by the Penguin Group
Penguin Young Readers Group, 345 Hudson Street, New York, New York 10014, U.S.A.
Penguin Group (Canada), 90 Eglinton Avenue East, Suite 700, Toronto, Ontario, Canada M4P 2Y3 (a division of Pearson Penguin Canada Inc.)
Penguin Books Ltd, 80 Strand, London WC2R 0RL, England
Penguin Ireland, 25 St Stephen's Green, Dublin 2, Ireland
(a division of Penguin Books Ltd)
Penguin Group (Australia), 250 Camberwell Road, Camberwell, Victoria 3124, Australia
(a division of Pearson Australia Group Pty Ltd)
Penguin Books India Pvt Ltd, 11 Community Centre, Panchsheel Park, New Delhi - 110 017, India
Penguin Group (NZ), 67 Apollo Drive, Rosedale, North Shore 0632, New Zealand (a division of Pearson New Zealand Ltd)
Penguin Books (South Africa) (Pty) Ltd, 24 Sturdee Avenue, Rosebank, Johannesburg 2196, South Africa

Registered Offices: Penguin Books Ltd, 80 Strand, London WC2R 0RL, England

First published in the United States of America by Viking, a division of Penguin Young Readers Group, 2007
Published by Puffin Books, a division of Penguin Young Readers Group, 2009

5 7 9 10 8 6 4

THE LIBRARY OF CONGRESS HAS CATALOGED THE VIKING EDITION AS FOLLOWS:
Carlson, Nancy L.
I don't like to read! / written and illustrated by Nancy Carlson.
p. cm.
Summary: Henry the mouse likes everything about first grade except reading, but with some extra help at school and home, he is delightfully surprised.
ISBN: 978-0-670-06191-4 (hc)
[1. Reading—Fiction. 2. Books and Reading—Fiction. 3. Mice—Fiction.] I. Title. II. Title: I do not like to read!
PZ7.C21665Iaam 2007 [E]—dc22 2006029072

Puffin Books ISBN 978-0-14-241451-4

Manufactured in China

Set in Avenir
Book design by Sam Kim

Henry was now in first grade,

and he was learning lots of new things!

But there was one thing Henry did not like about
first grade . . .

READING!

It seemed like everyone else liked to read . . .
especially Tony,

who bragged that he could read his favorite
book upside down.

Henry really liked listening to stories at school

and at home.

But when Mr. McCarthy asked if anyone
wanted to read,

Henry never raised his hand.
"Reading is boring!" he said.

At home, whenever Henry was asked to read,

he said, "No. I don't like to read! It's dumb!"

One day after school, Mr. McCarthy asked
Henry, "Why don't you like to read?"

"Because all the words and letters

just don't make any sense!" cried Henry.

"That's okay, Henry. Everyone learns to read in their own way," said Mr. McCarthy. "With a little extra help, soon *you'll* be reading!"

Still, Henry wasn't so sure he
would *ever* like to read.

But Henry started getting extra help with his
reading at school . . .

and made special time for reading at home.

Pretty soon some letters and words

around him started to make sense.

One night, Henry and Pete's babysitter
was reading them a brand-new library book.

But just as she got to the best
part, her friend called!

And she would not stop talking!

Pete really wanted to know what was going to happen in the story. "Henry, can you read it to me?" he asked.

"Well, I really don't like to read, but I'll try," said Henry.

The letters started coming together into words, and before he knew it, Henry had read all the way to the end!

He liked reading it so much, he read Pete another one!

The next day at school, when Mr. McCarthy asked,
"Who wants to read the lunch menu?". . .

Henry was the first to raise his hand!